KALEIDOSCOPE

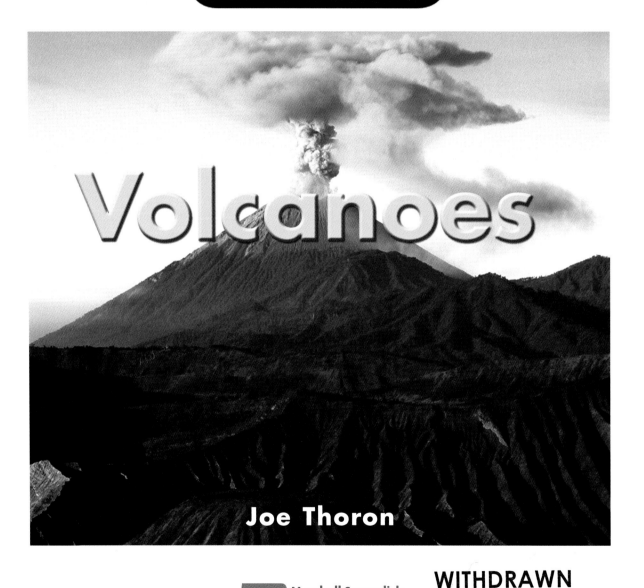

Volcanoes

Joe Thoron

Marshall Cavendish Benchmark
New York

Marshall Cavendish Benchmark
99 White Plains Road
Tarrytown, New York 10591-9001
www.marshallcavendish.us

Library of Congress Cataloging-in-Publication Data
Thoron, Joe.
Volcanoes / by Joe Thoron.
p. cm. — (Kaleidoscope)
Includes bibliographical references and index.
ISBN-13: 978-0-7614-2105-4
ISBN-10: 0-7614-2105-X
1. Volcanoes—Juvenile literature. I. Title. II. Series: Kaleidoscope (Tarrytown, N.Y.)
QE521.3.T55 2006   551.21—dc22   2005025838

Editor: Marilyn Mark
Editorial Director: Michelle Bisson
Art Director: Anahid Hamparian
Series Designer: Adam Mietlowski

Photo Research by Anne Burns Images
Cover Photo by Corbis/Gary Braasch

The photographs in this book are used with permission and through the courtesy of: *Corbis*: p. 1, 19 Sigit Pamungkas/Reuters; p. 12
Gavriel Jecan; p. 20 W. Perry Conway; p. 27 Japan Coast Guard/Handout/Reuters; p. 35 Michael S. Yamashita; p. 39 Jacques
Langevin/Sygma; p. 40 Roger Ressmeyer *NOAA*: pp. 4, 7 *USGS*: p. 8 Lyn Topinka; p. 23 B. Chouet, p. 24 R. McGimsey; p. 28 E. Wolfe *Photo
Researchers, Inc.*: p. 11 Gary Hincks; p. 15 Henning Dalhoff/Bonnier Pub. *Science Photo Library*: p. 16 Gary Hincks; p. 31, 36 Jeremy Bishop;
p. 43 Tony Craddock *Bridgeman Art Library*: p. 32 Private Collection

Printed in Malaysia

6 5 4 3 2 1

Contents

A Mountain Blown Apart

On March 20, 1980, several minor earthquakes shook the ground on the northern flank of Mount St. Helens, located in Washington State. Two days later, steam blew from a new crater at the summit of the 9,677-foot (2,949-meter) mountain. Over the next month the crater grew, and a column of gas and *ash* rose several miles into the air above it. At the same time, the north side of the mountain bulged like an expanding balloon. Some areas moved outward as much as 328 feet (100 m). Scientists knew an eruption would happen soon, but they did not know when.

A crater forms at the top of Mount St. Helens in late March 1980.

Then, on May 18, it happened. An earthquake on the mountain triggered two huge landslides, and the mountain exploded, shooting a mixture of steam and ash northward at speeds of more than 600 miles (966 kilometers) per hour. Next, the volcano erupted straight upward, sending a cloud of debris, or dirt and dust, 16 miles (26 km) into the atmosphere.

The south face of Mount St. Helens during the height of the May 18, 1980, eruption. Steam and ash float upward from the crater and larger fragments fall from the cloud. ▷

Dust and ash rained down on cities and towns in Washington and Oregon. The forests around the mountain were knocked flat, and a ring of devastation surrounded the once quiet peak, which was now almost 1,313 feet (400 m) shorter. More than fifty people died. The main explosion lasted about five minutes, but the vent continued to spew ash into the air for another nine hours.

Volcanic ash from the 1980 Mount St. Helens eruption fell in eleven states. Here, a helicopter lands, stirring up nearby ash.

What Is a Volcano?

A volcano is a vent in Earth's crust that lets *magma*—molten rock contained at high pressure within the Earth—reach the surface. The word "volcano" also describes a mountain created by eruptions of *lava* and rock.

Some volcanoes are active. Some are extinct. Some are asleep. An active volcano is one that has erupted sometime in the past 10,000 years. An extinct volcano is one that has not erupted for several hundred thousand years, and will probably never erupt again. A sleeping, or dormant, volcano is active but not currently erupting. A volcano is "erupting" if it is ejecting lava or solid fragments of rock.

Cutaway diagram of the eruption of a volcano. ▶

Some active volcanoes, such as Mauna Loa volcano in Hawaii, have short periods of dormancy ranging from a few months to twenty-five years. Other volcanoes sleep for many thousands of years between eruptions. Often the volcanoes that sleep the longest erupt the most violently when they finally wake up. Scientists determine the *repose time*—the time between eruptions—through written records or by carefully dating the evidence of past events.

Mauna Loa volcano on the island of Hawaii is an active volcano.

What Causes Volcanoes?

Volcanoes are caused by heat within the Earth and by the movement of Earth's *crust.*

The ground beneath your feet may seem solid and stationary, but the Earth's crust is only a thin skin over a ball of semimolten rock. The crust is about 20 to 25 miles (32–40 km) thick under the continents and about 3 miles (5 km) thick under the oceans. Beneath the crust is a thick layer of rock called the *mantle.* The mantle is about 1,800 miles (2,897 km) thick. It is made up of very hot rocks, some of which are solid and some of which are liquid. The Earth's core, made up of liquid and solid iron, is beneath the mantle.

Cutaway illustration of Earth, showing the crust, three layers of mantle, and the outer and inner core. ▶

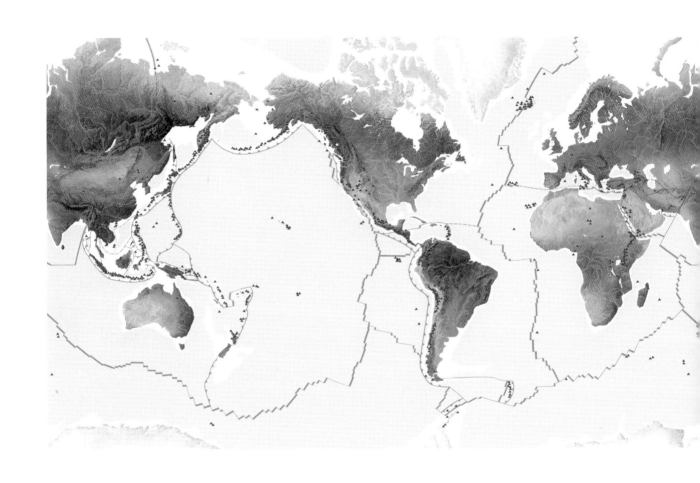

16

Near the crust, the mantle is about 1,300 degrees Fahrenheit (705 degrees Celsius)—hot enough to melt some of the rocks in the crust, which form magma. Near Earth's core, the temperature can reach 7,000 degrees F (3,871 degrees C). Temperature differences within the mantle cause the semimolten rock to move. Hotter rocks are lighter, and as they move toward the Earth's surface, they push other parts of the mantle out of the way. This movement carries the Earth's crust with it, very slowly, as slowly as your fingernails grow.

The crust is made up of *tectonic plates*. These smash and grind against one another. Sometimes one plate is pushed under another, sometimes they scrape past each other, and sometimes they crumple together and create massive mountain ranges such as the Himalayas.

In this world map, the gray lines show Earth's tectonic plates. The red dots mark the locations of volcanoes.

Many of the Earth's volcanoes occur at the places where two plates meet. *Rift volcanoes* appear when plates separate, creating a crack where magma can well up. Most occur deep in the ocean. On land, the best known rift volcanoes are in Iceland.

Subduction volcanoes occur where one plate is forced underneath another. This happens along the western edge of North and South America, where the heavy oceanic plate dives underneath the lighter continental plate. Parts of the oceanic crust melt as the plate goes deeper into the Earth. The magma rises through cracks in the crust. Some of it cools into hard rock before reaching the surface, but some breaks through, creating volcanoes. The *Ring of Fire*—volcanoes that line both sides of the Pacific Ocean—are all subduction volcanoes.

Mount Bromo in Indonesia erupts. Indonesia is part of the "Ring of Fire" and has more than one hundred active volcanoes.

Some volcanoes, such as those on the Hawaiian Islands, occur in the middle of a tectonic plate rather than at the edge. They are over a *hot spot*, or a place where hot magma rises straight up from deep within Earth. The hot spot stays in one place while the crust moves slowly over it. Five million years ago, the Hawaiian island of Kauai was located where the Big Island is now. The Hawaiian hot spot has been active in the same place for about 75 million years.

Yellowstone National Park in Wyoming sits over another hot spot.

The Grand Geyser at Yellowstone National Park in Wyoming sits over a hot spot.

Types of Volcanic Eruptions

There are six basic kinds of volcanic eruptions: Icelandic, Hawaiian, Strombolian, Vulcanian, Pelean, and Plinian.

Icelandic and Hawaiian volcanoes are the least explosive. They release lava that flows out in sheets or rivers. The other types are increasingly more violent.

Volcanoes erupt differently because of the different kinds of magma that drive them. Magma is not just rock. It has dissolved gases in it, and some magma rocks have more gases than others.

Strombolian eruptions can create beautiful fountains of molten lava fragments.

Dissolved gases are like the carbon dioxide in a soda bottle. Under pressure, these gases are squeezed down to a fraction of the space they normally take up. When you open a bottle of soda you release the pressure, and the dissolved carbon dioxide expands into little bubbles. The same thing happens when magma reaches the surface. If the magma is more liquid, as it is in Hawaii, the gases bubble out without causing explosions. If the magma is more rocklike, as at Mount St. Helens, the sudden release of pressure causes the molten rock to explode violently.

Plinian eruptions, such as this one seen in Alaska in 1992, send huge, dark columns of rock and gas high into the atmosphere.

Another factor in volcanic explosions is the effect of superheated groundwater. The high pressure underground causes water below the Earth's surface to reach temperatures of more than 212 degrees F (100 degrees C), water's normal boiling point, without boiling. If the pressure suddenly releases, the water changes into steam and expands violently, fueling an explosive eruption.

Underwater volcanoes in the deep ocean rarely erupt violently. This is because the weight of the water above keeps the pressure on the magma from changing and prevents the dissolved gases from expanding rapidly.

An underwater volcano erupts in the Pacific Ocean near Minami Iwojima Island, south of Tokyo, Japan.

Volcanic Ash and Debris

When a volcano erupts explosively, materials such as dust, ash, gases, and lava are released. All of the rocks, large and small, ejected from a volcano are called *tephra*.

Volcanic ash consists of fragments of volcanic rock less than one-tenth of an inch (0.2 cm) in diameter. Ash particles are carried away from the volcano vent by the wind. The largest and heaviest pieces drop to the ground first. The finer ones travel farther before settling to the ground. Ash can blanket large areas and make soil fertile as it slowly decomposes.

Volcanic ash rains down following the explosion of Mount Pinatubo in the Philippines. The ash creates an eerie darkness.

Larger chunks ejected from volcanoes are called *cinders*, and anything larger than a baseball is a *block* or a *bomb*. Blocks are chunks of rock that were solid before the eruption. Bombs are globs of new magma (lava) that fly through the air still hot and glowing. Sometimes blocks and bombs can land a great distance from the volcano.

In extremely violent eruptions, volcanic dust (particles smaller than one-sixteenth of a millimeter) and tiny droplets of volcanic gas and water can be thrown into the *stratosphere*. Once these particles reach this height, they stay there for months or years, circling the globe and affecting world weather patterns.

This lava block was thrown into the air by a steam explosion at the Kilauea volcano in Hawaii.

Pyroclastic Flows, Avalanches, and Mudflows

Some of a volcano's most dangerous and damaging effects do not come from the force of the initial blast. They come from flowing mud and from avalanches of rocks and other hot debris.

In some eruptions, glowing clouds of hot volcanic rock fragments and gases sweep down the sides of the volcano. The mixtures are heavier than air, so they hug the ground. These are called *pyroclastic flows*. The Italian towns of Pompeii and Herculaneum were overwhelmed by pyroclastic flows when Mount Vesuvius erupted in 79 CE.

A nineteenth-century depiction of the destruction of Pompeii, painted by Antonio Niccolini (1772–1850).

Sometimes the flows are formed by sideways blasts out of the mountain. Other times a pyroclastic flow is formed when material falls out of the ash cloud because it is too heavy to stay airborne. Temperatures in a pyroclastic flow can be as high as 1,652 degrees F (900 degrees C), and the material can move over the ground at speeds of as much as 124 mph (200 kph).

This man must crouch to walk through his front door. Pyroclastic flow from the Unzen volcano in Japan filled half of his house with ash and debris, which later hardened.

Debris avalanches of rock, snow, and ice sometimes occur in volcanic eruptions. At Mount St. Helens, a huge chunk of the mountain slid off to the north. It swept 14 miles (23 km) down the valley of the Toutle River, leaving deposits of rock and debris about 148 feet (45 m) deep on average and 656 feet (200 m) deep in some places. Before the Mount St. Helens eruption, scientists did not know much about debris avalanches. Since then, though, they have found evidence of other past avalanches. For example, a debris avalanche at Mount Shasta in California some 300,000 years ago was about eight times larger than the one at Mount St. Helens.

A volcanologist in a heat suit takes samples near a lava flow on Mount Etna in Sicily. Volcanologists are scientists who study volcanoes.

Mudflows present a different danger. They often occur hours after an eruption. Many volcanoes, even the ones near the equator, are tall enough to be covered in a blanket of snow and ice. The heat of an eruption can melt the ice and snow, releasing a large volume of water. This water mixes with any volcanic ash that has already fallen and creates a river of mud.

Mudflows, also called "lahars" (an Indonesian word), sweep down river valleys and cause great destruction. On November 13, 1985, an entire town in Colombia was destroyed by a mudflow when the Nevado del Ruiz volcano erupted. The snow and ice from high on the mountain swept down a canyon at about 22 mph (35 kph), gathering rocks, trees, and soil as it went. The mudflow reached the town of Armero within two hours and killed about 22,000 people.

The town of Armero, Colombia, was destroyed by the eruption of the Nevado del Ruiz volcano.

Preventing Death and Destruction

Predicting volcanic eruptions is not an exact science. Often, scientists look at a volcano's history since many volcanoes erupt on a somewhat regular basis.

Scientists also monitor the underground activity near a volcano. Volcanoes erupt after magma moves close to the surface, shifting the surrounding earth out of the way. Sometimes the ground bulges up. Also, the chemical composition of the crater's fumes can change. Still, it is almost impossible to predict exactly when a major eruption will take place.

In most cases, the only way to stay safe when a volcano erupts is to stay out of the way. No one can outrun an avalanche, mudflow, or pyroclastic flow.

This hole reveals molten lava flowing inside a lava tube near Kilaeua, Hawaii, in Volcanoes National Park. Volcanologists will study this lava.

So why do people live near volcanoes? One reason is that volcanic soil is some of the best soil in the world. Ash deposits provide rich nutrients for crops. Also, volcanoes don't erupt often, and it is easy for people to think that the danger is not real.

Predictions of eruptions are always a bit vague, and it is hard for people to know whether or not to evacuate. Government officials should calculate and understand the real risks and dangers for their area before an eruption occurs. Then they can have safety plans based on sound science already in place.

If you live near a volcano, educate yourself about that mountain's history. The chances are good that the mountain will not erupt in your lifetime. If it does start to come back to life, make an emergency plan with your family so you will know how to stay safe.

Flowers thrive near Mount St. Helens only twenty years after the 1980 blast. ▶

Glossary

ash—Small fragments of lava or rock formed by volcanic eruptions.

block—A solid rock 2.5 inches (6.4 cm) or more in diameter that is ejected from a volcano.

bomb—A chunk of lava 2.5 inches (6.4 cm) or more in diameter that is ejected from a volcano.

cinders—Lava fragments about half an inch (1 cm) in diameter. Also called "scoria."

crust—The solid outer layer of the Earth.

debris avalanches—Masses of rock, snow, and ice that slide off a mountain during a volcanic eruption.

hot spot—A stationary area of high heat within the mantle.

lava—Molten rock on the surface of the Earth; magma that has reached the surface.

magma—Molten rock below the surface of Earth.

mantle—The semimolten layer of Earth above the core and below the crust.

mudflow—A mix of water, mud, and debris that flows downhill. Also called "lahars."

pyroclastic flows—Clouds of hot ash and gases that sweep down from a volcano.

repose time—The time between eruptions of an active volcano.

rift volcano—A volcano located where two tectonic plates are separating and new crust is being created.

Ring of Fire—The region of volcanoes lining the Pacific Ocean where oceanic crust is being forced underneath continental crust.

stratosphere—A layer of the upper atmosphere.

subduction volcano—A volcano located inland from an area where one tectonic plate is being forced underneath another.

tectonic plates—Portions of the Earth's crust that move slowly across the globe.

tephra—A general name for all the material that erupts from a volcano.

45

Find Out More

Books

Bunce, Vincent J. *Volcanoes*. Austin, TX: Raintree Steck-Vaughn, 2000.
Green, Jen. *Volcanoes*. Brookfield, CT: Copper Beech, 1998.
Rogers, Daniel. *Volcanoes*. Austin, TX: Raintree Steck-Vaughn, 1999.

Web Sites

The Federal Emergency Management Agency (FEMA) for Kids
http://www.fema.com/kids/volcano.htm

The United States Geological Survey (USGS)
http://volcanoes.usgs.gov/

Volcano Adventure Tours
http://www.volcanolive.com/

About the Author

Joe Thoron is a freelance writer in Washington State. When not writing for children, he builds Web sites and writes marketing copy. He lives on an island north of Seattle, right between several sleeping volcanoes and a major earthquake zone.

Index

Page numbers for illustrations are in **boldface**.